CURLIES

COLOR TOO

CURLIES COLOR TOO focuses on teaching our young girls that natural is beautiful. Some may think its "just hair" but accepting our natural selves including our hair are all apart of the bigger picture, "self love"! Teaching our young girls to love their natural hair is just the beginning to them being confident in this world that constantly promotes long, straight hair. It is critical that we nuture them with entertainment and learning tools that have illustrations that look like "us".

This coloring book is not only for your little one but its for Mothers as well. This is a hairstyle look book too! Each illustration has a hairstyle for your little one to choose as their "hairstyle of the day"!

M♥MMY&ME

For my Taylor & Skylar bears-
the inspiration behind my passion
to educate mothers to teach
their children to ♥
themselves- hair & all!

To all my curlfriends who show me
continuous love & support!
The natural hair community has
been amazing to me! X○

Yolanda Renee

"IT'S MORE THAN JUST HAIR" VS "IT'S JUST HAIR"

We've all heard the infamous quotes "it's more than just hair" and "its just hair, gosh!" Ironically, they both make sense. It is just hair on the surface but society plays an immense role into it becoming something more. Society constantly pushes long, straight, luscious, non-frizzy hair through TV shows, movies, magazines, books, advertisements, and list goes on. Not only do they push those views on the masses but they also "throw shade" on African American's natural hair. At this point, it becomes more than just hair. We are in a competition with a major challenger to teach our sistas otherwise. It's sad to hear that young children are being expelled from school for wearing eccentric African American hairstyles to school, women being treated unfairly at work for rocking a fierce afro, and even our men not getting their dream job because their dreadlocks are not deemed as professional. Most importantly when our young daughters come home from school telling Mommy she wants long, straight, light colored hair like little Susie! This is exactly when "it's more than just hair".

As Mothers it is our duty to fight against society's views on our natural hair. Not only to show the world that our natural hair is beautiful but to reach deeper within our children and teach them self love, respect, and confidence. Oh you may be saying those exact words right now, "its just hair" but this hair is a gateway to other things- it can go in a positive direction or a negative one, and let's make sure those "other things" are going in the right direction.

BREAKING THE CYCLE

While attending middle and high school I remember being extremely jealous of some of my classmates that had long, thick, frizzy hair. There were only a few- I can count them on one hand because even then most black girls had relaxers. Having a relaxer was almost like a reward, a milestone in our life. It's sad to say, but once you reached a certain age you knew a perm was coming. Until now I did not realize how brainwashed I was about natural hair and relaxers. Seeing those few girls with their beautiful hair, I thought to myself, "They must have that 'good hair' because it looks like that without a relaxer!" I even thought their parents were too strict because they would not allow them to get a perm until they were adults (like they were missing out on something, lol, NOT!). I even thought my hair was horrible because I had to get a perm and my hair could never look like theirs. The cycle is so deep that despite all my inner thoughts and questions I still took over my relaxer regimen when I was old enough to do so. Why did I continue to perm my hair? It is because we do what our parents do, from childhood into adulthood with little to no thought. We can use that to our advantage but we will get into that a little later.

I personally do not remember getting my first relaxer. Do you? Not remembering is a clear indicator that I was very young, most likely in kindergarten or 1st grade which is scary because I cannot imagine giving my daughter, Taylor (5 years old) a perm at this age. Parents nowadays are even more eager to straighten their daughter's hair because they are excited to see how straight it will be, how long it is, and they basically want a break from caring for it. Some parents are so deep in the cycle that it is a rule in their household that natural hair is not allowed. Yaaaassss! You read that correctly. I recently read an article about a young girl with a relaxer who suddenly wanted to grow her natural hair but she was forbidden by her Mother. There was an outrage on social media platforms about this controversy. This is when I look deeper into what our role is as a parent. I've heard this from my Mother plenty of times during my childhood, "as long as you are living under my roof, MY RULES OR GET OUT!" I'm sure you heard something similar plenty of times. Lol. But not allowing your daughter to rock her natural hair is going a little too far, don't you think? Let's think of some of the reasons parents use relaxers, (1) they want their daughter to have straight hair, (2) Mothers need a break from taking care of "all that hair", (3) its just easier! Rebuttal time! Those are the usual responses, right? With natural hair you can straighten it as long as your do it properly to eliminate heat damage. Taking care of natural hair can be challenging however, if you need a break from it protective styling will be your savior! Protective styling can last 1-2 weeks with proper care and refreshing. And finally, it may be easier but what lesson are you teaching your child by doing it because it's easier? I mean, we all have heard the quote, "work smarter, not harder!" But for real, that does not apply to our natural hair. There are easier ways to care for your natural hair but a relaxer is not the answer. Learning the proper regimen and using the right products is the key to that quote. You can work smarter by still having natural hair! I don't put all blame on Mothers because again the cycle is so deep they don't know anything else. They know that their Mother had a relaxer who then gave them a relaxer and it's their job to keep up with the tradition, lol! Knowledge is key and to learn about natural hair you definitely have jump in there aggressively to get the knowledge. Even with natural hair trending around the world it is still difficult to learn about natural hair because there are so many different textures, products, regimens, resources, etc. A perfect example is my cousins Tynika and Loleta! They are going to kill me for writing about them in this book! Lol. We all attended our grandmother's birthday party at the nursing home and of course natural hair came up because I walked in with a huge mega puff! And they know I love natural hair! I noticed Tynika's daughter who is 5 years old had bone straight hair! I almost lost it- I asked Tynika did she perm her hair and she replied she had a texturizer put in her hair! She explained that her daughter's hair was just too much to deal with. I asked her a few questions like, why didn't you call me first? What products are you using on her hair? Do you have a regimen? I wanted to get to the root of the problem and know everything! We talked about it for a few minutes and I tried to help her but she had an answer aka "an excuse" for everything. I felt like I was not getting anywhere with her about the issues she was having with her daughter's natural hair. After awhile I thought I broke ice! Yesssssssss, finally she gets it! Then Tynika says to me, "no matter what I do to her hair I just cannot get her hair STRAIGHT!" OMG! *pause* Curlfriends, I think I fainted when she said that! But then I came back to life because that statement coming out of her mouth was so genuine and she had no clue what she was saying. She honestly felt as though she had failed at caring for her daughter's hair because she could not get it straight. That moment was so powerful to me because she is just like the many Mothers out here who do not know a thing about natural hair. They are so brainwashed by society and our own cycle of perming our hair that she really thought the goal was to get straight hair instead of healthy curly , coily, kinky hair! Just imagine how Mothers feel defeated because they are fighting the wrong battle. They are settling for a relaxer because they feel like they are not able to properly take care of their children's hair because they think its supposed to be straight instead of curly.

Initially, I started my Mommy & Me seminar to present at natural hair events just as refresher for naturalistas and their daughters but after this conversation my efforts are to reach Mothers like my cousins Tynika and Loleta. As naturals we do struggle with our own natural hair because we have something to compare it to. We had relaxers at one point, transitioned or big chopped and then learned how to take care of our natural hair. So it can be a struggle when you compare it to your "relaxer life"! And then some naturals have no problem with their natural texture but may have a daughter with a completely different texture, and are struggling with it. That naturalista may be on the brink of putting a relaxer in their daughter's hair for that very reason. So presenting my seminar does touch those naturalistas...but what about the Mothers who are not natural who do not attend natural hair events. They need help from us! I'm telling you, the cycle is crazy DEEP yall! So deep that those Mothers are presenting relaxers as a milestone, a reward, and like we've touched on previously, a requirement or rule of the house!

As parents we do set rules and regulations and assign chores, curfews, etc as a tool to mold our children into mature, responsible, loving, successful adults, correct? Having them clean their room and make their beds every morning is teaching them to take care of their space. Making them work on their homework and studying regularly is preparing them for higher learning, right? The list goes on. Overall rules should have a purpose behind them. But not allowing your daughter to rock her natural hair absolutely does not have a purpose behind it. And certainly making your daughter get her first perm is not setting a good example either. Instead of looking forward to the perfect age to put a relaxer in her hair, we as Mothers should be celebrating that age to see if our hard work of showing her how beautiful her natural hair is has taught her self love overall. To me the few girls I remember from high school with natural hair had parents who were breaking the cycle of relaxing our natural hair. Whether they knew it or not, they were touching others not just their children. It may have taken me a decade to learn the lesson but now that I am natural I am ready to break the cycle starting with my two daughters, Taylor and Skylar. They love their natural hair because they love to be just like Mommy! But as they grow older this may change and I am prepared for it. Like my classmates' parents, I am at least going to make sure my girls keep their natural hair until they graduate high school. By then they will be properly educated on how to care for their natural hair as well as informed about relaxers. Once they are young adults they can make their own decision. I feel strongly about parents making this decision for their child; it should most definitely be something your child should be able to decide without having to big chop. Remember, it's more than just hair. Your daughter loving her hair will be a gateway to loving each and every thing about herself, even if it's different than what society puts in front of us. But if we conform and push her to get a relaxer to fit in, she may try to fit in by changing other things about herself- even to an extreme of bleaching her skin. Let's break the cycle- don't make them get a perm because you got a perm at age 6, your Mother had one at the age of 7, and so on. Let's start a new cycle and give our girls a chance to fall in love with their natural hair.

IT IS MORE THAN JUST HAIR

After that never ending lecture you are most likely thinking, "Okay already, how do I get my daughter to love her natural hair?" Whether you are #teamnatural or not, I feel like it is a Mother's duty to help her embrace her natural hair into adulthood. The first suggestion may be hard for Mothers who are not natural but there are some ways around it.

SUGGESTION #1 | LOVE YOUR NATURAL

Daughters want to be just like Mommy, right? Make sure she is watching when you are in the bathroom mirror checking out your bangin' bantu knot out! Or do a" hair flip" with that ahhhhmazing twistout, and then give her a quick smile. Seriously, showing her that you love your natural hair is the best way to teach your daughter without actually having a sit down lesson about it; these small instances will grow on her. If you as a parent do not have natural hair you can still rock natural hair styles which will also influence your children in a positive way. There are several options such as poetic justice braids, kinky twists, afro textures weaves and wigs, corn rows, and more. These styles also showcase the versatility of our natural hair.

SUGGESTION #2 | HAVE A REGIMEN

The first rule you learn as a Mother is, a schedule is key to having a happy baby! Babies like everything to be planned out for them. This allows them to learn what is happening on a daily basis! They absolutely do not like surprises or things being out of order. This same rule goes for caring for natural hair. You have a feeding schedule, bath time, reading time, etc. Now let's add natural hair time! The regimen should be on the same day and time. I say this because you do not want to randomly start wash day an hour before you go to church, a family reunion, or to go out shopping, etc. If you decide to start wash day randomly most likely it's not going to be a good time. Rushing may be involved which will then follow up with pulling and tugging your daughter's hair, huffing and puffing of frustration, maybe even an occasional smack of the hands with a comb or brush! I remember those days! Having a set schedule will eliminate any negative factors which is key to helping your daughter love her natural hair. If you show any negativity while carrying out wash day this will discourage her to keep up with the regimen. We do not want give off a vibe that natural hair is too much to deal with. Just take your time with the regimen and make it a fun bonding experience.

Wash Day in my household is BATHING SUIT DAY! YAYYYY! Taylor and Skylar wear their favorite bathing suit and they are ready to get soaking wet with water, shampoo and conditioner! That eliminates the stress of not getting the towel or her clothes wet. You might as well throw that out the window! Wash day is going to get messy! We have fun with it. I wash my girls' hair in the shower on a bar stool. Taylor and Skylar are allowed to help with the process by adding products and detangling their own section of hair! Allowing them to help will keep them interested and occupied . It will also help them learn how to care for their hair by themselves. Taylor is the oldest and at the age of 5 she knows how to detangle her own hair and she can tell you all the products that work for her hair and what they are used for. And again, I did not teach her this in a lesson format. Over the years she just paid attention and naturally learned her own regimen. I can see Skylar learning the very same way (she's only 3 right now). Overall, have a set regimen, remain positive, and bond with your child!

SUGGESTION #3 | KEEP IT INTERESTING WITH DIFFERENT NATURAL HAIR STYLES

The best way to keep your daughter interested is beautiful hairstyles! You have to switch it up because the best thing about natural hair is its versatility! We can rock it in its afro state, twists, braids, crimpy, pinned up, and even straight. There are so many different styles, for example:

1. PUFF
2. BUN
3. PONYTAILS
4. BRAIDS
5. CORN ROWS
6. TWO STRAND TWISTS
7. BANTU KNOTS
8. FRENCH BRAIDS
9. BRAIDED MOHAWK
10. AFRO PUFFS
11. MINI TWISTS
12. PIGTAILS
13. TWIST OUT
14. BRAID OUT
15. BAIDED BUN
16. FRO-HAWK

And even with those basic styles there are so many variations and combinations you can do! The possibilities are endless. On those days when you daughter asks to rock her hair straight- guess what, you can straighten natural hair. Showing your daughter all these options will definitely teach her the versatility of natural hair.

SUGGESTION #4 | SURROUND HER WITH LEARNING & ENTERTAINMENT THAT LOOKS LIKE "US"

As a young girl reading and observing girls that look like "us" with darker skin and big frizzy hair means the world to them! Whether it's on their favorite cartoon, reading book, coloring book, or in a movie; this helps them understand that they are worthy. It helps with self esteem and self love. You can gradually build their library with fun books with curly girls in them. I have a list of Children's Book for you at the end of this book. And don't forget to add this coloring book to her library too!

There are tons of creative ways for you to reach your daughter about self love and her natural hair. Some may have a more difficult challenge than others. Understand that we as Mothers have to unite to break the cycle of changing our hair to fit in with society. We need to learn and love our natural hair to show the world that it is beautiful, versatile, professional, and acceptable. Just imagine if your daughter loves her hair- that self love and confidence will touch another young girl and it will have a ripple effect. That is the cycle that needs to be in our community- a cycle of positivity that uplifts others around you, starting with JUST HAIR.

MOMMY & ME

This book is for both, Mommy & Me and I hope this part of the book, "MOMMY" has inspired someone to continue our new cycle- our new journey. The rest of the book is for your daughters, the "ME" part of the book. You will find several curlie girls with different hairstyles, earrings that will help them learn their shapes, and several learning activities. Keep the book handy because on those days you don't feel like picking out a hairstyle to do for the week, let your little one pick one from this book!

BEADED CORNROWS

LETTERS

A B C D E

F G H I J K

L M N O P

Q R S T U

V W X Y Z

_____

(YOUR NAME)

BRAIDED PONYTAIL

SOCK BUN

BRAIDED PUFFS

SHAPES

TAKE A CLOSE LOOK AT THE CURLY
GIRLS' EARRINGS AND DRAW A LINE
TO THE MATCHING SHAPES.

DREADS

BRAIDED AFRO

NUMBERS

COUNT EACH GROUP OF CURLIESOUT LOUD AND THEN TRACE THE NUMBERS!

1

2

3

4

5

6

A PUFF

PONYTAILS

PIGTAILS

CORNROWS

WORDSEARCH

HAVE MOMMY HELP YOU FIND THE WORDS!

BABY HAIR
BARRETTES
BRAIDS
BRUSH
COMB
CORNROWS
CURLY
FRIZZY

HAIR BEADS
NATURAL HAIR
PONYTAILS
PUFFS
TEAM NATURAL
TWISTOUT
WASH DAY
BANTU KNOTS

```
U Y U F H X O H S U R B H S W
K S S H I S D I A R B G U K S
N T F T H R Y U B E I S R D T
P O Q D Z I T J H Q P W A Y A
K N M C P A K F R R K E K J I
W K C T B H R L P R B T B C R
U U U O A L J U P R X E I W T
A T R P R A V U I I A A B P W
L N L K R R W A B A W M B V I
L A Y B E U H T W A Y N A N S
P B J M T T Q Y S Z P A B G T
R Y T O T A O H Z M U T Y D O
T V W C E N D I Q G F U H P U
S I R F S A R A Q S F R A T T
A C Q I Y F Z T W B S A I L D
R L J C O R N R O W S L R J R
```

A BIG BOW

CURLIES
COLOR TOO
by Yolanda Renee

A COLORING & HAIR STYLE BOOK

 MOMMY&ME by Yolanda Dove

CURLY GIRL CHILDREN'S BOOKS:

Curlie's Fun With Bubbles By Sherry Bodie

I Love My Hair by Natasha Anastasia Tarpley and EB Lewis

Please, Baby, Please by Spike Lee, Tonya Lewis Lee and Kadir Nelson

Dancing in the Wings by Debbie Allen and Kadir Nelson

Girl of Mine by Jabari Asim and LeUyen Pham

Keena Ford and the Second Grade Mix Up by Melissa Thomson

Please, Puppy, Please by Spike Lee

One Crazy Summer by Rita Williams-Garcia

Peekaboo Morning by Rachel Isadora

Sugar Pum Ballerinas by Whoopi Goldberg...

One Love by Cedella Marley and Vanessa Newton

Happy to Be Nappy by Bell Hooks and Chris Raschka

Nappy Hair by Carolivia Herron

Homemade Love: Picture Book

I Like Myself! By Karen Beaumont

Please Baby Please by Spike Lee

Bintou's Braids by Sylvianne Diouf

Marvelous Me: Inside and Out by Lisa Bullard

I Love My Cotton Candy Hair by Nicole Updegraff

CHILDREN'S HAIR STYLES:

PUFF	CORN ROWS	BRAIDED MOHAWK	TWIST OUT
BUN	TWO STRAND TWISTS	AFRO PUFFS	BRAID OUT
PONYTAILS	BANTU KNOTS	MINI TWISTS	BRAIDED BUN
BRAIDS	FRENCH BRAID(S)	PIGTAILS	FRO-HAWK

CHILDREN'S NATURAL HAIR PRODUCTS:

MIXED CHICKS KIDS
JASON NATURAL KIDS ONLY SHAMPOO
FAIRY TALES CURLY-Q
CURLY Q'S COCONUT DREAM MOISTURIZING CONDITIONER
CURLY Q CUSTARD
AFRICA'S BEST KIDS ORGANIC
MISS JESSIE'S BABY BUTTERCREME
NATURE'S BABY ORGANICS CONDITIONER & DETANGLER
BELLA B BEE GONE CRADLE CAP BABY SHAMPOO
SUAVE DETANGLING SPRAY
IT'S A CURL RING AROUND THE CURLIES LEAVE IN
IT'S A CURL PEAKABOO SHAMPOO
ITS'A CURL PATTY CAKE CONDITIONER
NATURE'S NATURAL CARROTT HAIR OIL WITH SHEA BUTTER AND VITAMIN E
CAROL'S DAUGHTER HAIR MILK
SHEA MOISTURE CO-WASH CONDITIONING CLEANSER
SHEA MOISTURE BABY
RAW SHEA BUTTER/CHAMOMILE/ARGAN OIL HEAD TO TOE WASH & SHAMPOC
RAW SHEA BUTTER OIL RUB
COCONUT & HIBISCUS EXTRA MOISTURIZING DETANGLER
COCONUT & HIBISCUS EXTRA NOURISHING CONDITIONER
COCONUT & HIBISCUS EXTRA NOURISHING SHAMPOO
CURLING BUTTER CREAM

MOMMY&ME *by yolanda Dove*

TAYLOR & SKYLAR'S REGIMEN:

1 WASH DAY | ONCE A MONTH
PRE-POO/SHAMPOO

Once a month I will wash their hair with shampoo.
Before I shampoo I will apply a pre-poo which is a
mixture of your favorite oils, warmed up. Place a plastic
cap on their head and leave in for 15 minutes. Rinse. I do this
process in the shower as stated before. Taylor and Sky get to wear their
bathing suits! I then add the shampoo and gently detangle, rake the product
through the hair. Once I feel that her hair is slightly detangled and clean,
I rinse out the shampoo. I usually use shampoo only one time. But if you need
to repeat, do so.

CONDITIONER

I follow up with a conditioner and allow it to sit in the hair for 15 minutes. Put
the hair in a high puff or cover with a plastic cap. Honestly, I use a Target or
Walmart bag. Lol.

DETANGLE

After 5 minutes you can start finger detangling the hair. I also use a Hair Bean
to assist. Start with your fingers first; use a wide tooth comb if you must; and
then the hair bean. Finger detangling is best but using the hair bean or
comb can help as well. After I detangle each section I twist that section to
make sure it stays detangled. After detangling there are usually 7 sections.
I keep them twisted and then rinse with the shower. As I rinse I will take the
twists out and allow the water pressure soak and weigh the hair down. I then
add a leave in conditioner and continue with the LOC method and styling
(see below for details).

2 CO WASH | EVERY TWO WEEKS OR AS NEEDED

Shea Moisture has an amazing co-wash that is gentle and natural enough
to use on your children's hair. It has a perfect slip and a slight lather. I
sometimes use a pre-poo before co-washing but usually a co-wash is more
than enough. I will co-wash only once and then follow the same steps as
wash day above.

TAYLOR & SKYLAR'S REGIMEN:

3 LOC METHOD

The LOC Method is very important to retain moisture.

> LIQUID/LEAVE IN,
> OIL,
> CREAM,
> OIL (optional).

I have noticed using an oil on top of the method will eliminate any white residue from the cream of your choice.

4 STYLING

I then chose a style and rock it out! The style will last 1-2 weeks. And of course you will need to add moisture as needed. Instead of doing the layering process of the LOC Method during the week I will put the LOC Method in a bottle. It's a spritz. In a spray bottle I add the following ingredients:

> 1 Water
> 2 Aloe Vera Juice
> 3 Oil
> 4 Conditioner

Whatever style your daughter is rocking, spray this spritz on her hair. If its braids spray and massage the scalp. If its ponytails you should release the hair, spritz, and put it back into a ponytail. If you want to detangle at this point you can. If not the hair should be ok until your next co-wash day.

5 BEDTIME

At bedtime its beneficial to teach your daughter to wear a scarf. Skylar will wear one but Taylor will not. So you can get satin pillow cases for them. If not, the hair should still be ok since most little girls wear set styles that won't mess up. You may find you will have to add moisture more often though.

CUTIES

AFRICA

keep calm

ITS JUST

FRIZZ

thank you!

I want to thank everyone who purchased this coloring & hairstyle book which is my first publication. I didn't want it to be too complicated...its really down to earth and just fun for both you and your daughter(s). To keep up with myself and my girls, Taylor & Skylar please subscribe, like, and follow us on my social networks:

YOUTUBE http://www.youtube.com/etcblogmag
INSTAGRAM http://www.instagram.com/etcblogmag or @etcblogmag
FACEBOOK http://www.facebook.com/etcblogmag
TWITTER http://www.twitter.com/etcblogmag or @etcblogmag
TUMBLR http://etcblogmag.tumblr.com
BLOG http://www.etcblogmag.com

SHOP NOW http://www.etceteraboutique.bigcartel.com

BOOKING

If you are interested in me hosting or making an appearance at your next event please send an email to, etc.yolandarenee@gmail.com to request my hosting package. This package will include all the seminars I offer such as Mommy & Me, Meet & Beat, and a Blogger seminar. Serious inquiries ONLY.

etc KiDS is now available on www.etcboutique.spreadshirt.com! Here you will find your favorite Et Cetera Boutique designs on baby, toddler, and children's tees.

KEEP CALM ITS JUST FRIZZ   FRIZZY HAIR DON'T CARE

FRIZZY HAIR (PINK)   NATURAL BARBIE   MOMMY & ME   CURLIES

I LOVE MY HAIR (PINK)   I LOVE MY HAIR (RED)

MOMMY & ME LOGO TEE

ABOUT THE AUTHOR/ILLUSTRATOR

Yolanda Renee is the creator of www.etcblogmag.com, a fashion, style, beauty & natural hair blog. The blog's popularity has allowed her to branch out to start her very popular YouTube channel, www.youtube.com/etcblogmag (with over 1 millions views and counting), and even a natural hair boutique, Et Cetera Boutique (www.etceteraboutique.bigcartel.com). Her first love of course, is graphic design. Yolanda Renee is currently the graphic designer for Necole Bitchie of www.necolebitchie.com; she's also done work for Jenell Stewart of www.kinkycurlycoilyme.com, Taren Guy (www.tarenguy.com), Tamar Braxton, AJ Johnson, and many more. She has also been featured on www.curlynikki.com, www.blackgirllonghair.com, Natura Magazine, www.sunshinesnaturalandlovingit.com, Natural Hair Daily, CurlBox, and more!

Since doing her big chop in May 2012, and now being a part of the natural hair community her passions have come to life. Now with a target audience she is able to use her talents to reach thousands of women around the world. Her latest project is a Mommy & Me seminar which targets mothers to help them take care of their daughter's natural hair. And one key point to helping our daughter's love their hair is to surround them with learning tools, books, movies and entertainment as a whole, with curly girls that look like them! That is how this coloring & style book came to life! This is her first book and there's more to come!

Keep up with Yolanda Renee on www.etcblogmag.com, www.instagram.com/etcblogmag, www.youtube.com/etcblogmag!

ISBN-10: 1492868736
ISBN-13: 978-1492868736

24923795R00023

Made in the USA
San Bernardino, CA
12 October 2015